Eloise and the Big Parade

KAY THOMPSON'S ELOISE

Eloise and the Big Parade

STORY BY Lisa McClatchy

ILLUSTRATED BY Tammie Lyon

Ready-to-Read

Simon Spotlight

New York   London   Toronto   Sydney   New Delhi

SIMON SPOTLIGHT

An imprint of Simon & Schuster Children's Publishing Division

1230 Avenue of the Americas, New York, NY 10020

First Simon Spotlight hardcover edition May 2017

First Aladdin Paperbacks edition May 2007

Copyright © 2007 by the Estate of Kay Thompson

All rights reserved, including the right of reproduction in whole or in part in any form.

"Eloise" and related marks are trademarks of the Estate of Kay Thompson.

SIMON SPOTLIGHT, READY-TO-READ, and colophon are registered

trademarks of Simon & Schuster, Inc.

For information about special discounts for bulk purchases, please contact Simon & Schuster

Special Sales at 1-866-506-1949 or business@simonandschuster.com.

The text of this book was set in Century Old Style.

Manufactured in the United States of America 0417 LAK

2 4 6 8 10 9 7 5 3 1

Library of Congress Control Number 2006933443

ISBN 978-1-4814-8819-8 (hc)

ISBN 978-1-4169-3523-0 (pbk)

I am Eloise.
I live in The Plaza Hotel.

Today is the
Fourth of July parade.

Nanny loves a good parade.
So do I.

"Eloise," Nanny says,
"we must wear red, white,
and blue."

I wear a blue dress.
And white shoes.
And a red bow.

Nanny and I sit
right up front.

The marching band
arrives first.

I pretend I can play
the tuba.
Weenie plays the flute.

"Sit down, Eloise,"
Nanny says.

The clowns throw candy.
I grab as much as I can.

Then I try to juggle.
So does Weenie.

"Eloise! Sit down!"
Nanny yells.

The floats are next.
This one
is from New Orleans!
They throw party beads!

I wear as many as I can.
So does Weenie.
We dance in the street.

"Sit down, Eloise!"
Nanny yells.

Here come
the mounted police!

My favorite is
the palomino.
Nanny likes
the dapple gray.

I offer one some candy.
"No, no, no, Eloise!"
Nanny says.

A big car drives by us.
"There's the queen
of the parade!"
Nanny says.

I pretend I am a queen.
My bow is a crown.
My beads are jewels.
My dress is a gown.

Another car drives by.
I climb on up.

"Which queen are you?"
the driver says.
"I am Queen of The Plaza!"
I say.

Oh I love, love, love parades!